THE AMAZING SPIDER-MAN 2

THE OSCORP FILES

Written By Brittany Candau

Based on the screenplay by Alex Kurtzman & Roberto Orci & Jeff Pinkner

Produced by Avi Arad and Matt Tolmach

Directed by Marc Webb

Illustrated by Andy Smith, Drew Geraci, and Pete Pantazis

OSCORP INDUSTRIES

MARVEL

NEW YORK · LOS ANGELES

© MARVEL marvelkids.com © 2014 CPII

Printed in the United States of America

First Edition

1 3 5 7 9 10 8 6 4 2

Library of Congress Catalog Card Number: 2013954895

G942-9090-6-14046

ISBN 978-1-4847-0051-8

OSCORP
INDUSTRIES

To Whom It May Concern:

The following report contains top secret logs, lab reports, e-mail records, surveillance images, and more—all used in the investigations performed by Oscorp Industries.

It specifically looks into the aftermath of the cross-species genetics experiments conducted by Dr. Curtis Connors. It also includes details on the seemingly relevant masked menace known as Spider-Man. As the implications of such experiments could prove to be disastrous for the company, it is imperative that we look into every possible liability.

You hold in your hands strictly confidential information to be used for the security of Oscorp Industries. Any and all leaks of these materials will be dealt with severely.

Sincerely,

Donald Menken

Donald Menken
Director of Operations
Oscorp Industries

OSCORP

INDUSTRIES

EXCERPT FROM PETER PARKER SURVEILLANCE LOG (YEAR ONE)—FOREST HILLS, QUEENS

After the messy incidents involving Richard Parker, Norman Osborn has requested that Oscorp security keep a close eye on Parker's ten-year-old son.

The subject, one Peter Parker, has been sent to live with his aunt and uncle, May and Ben Parker. They are now the boy's legal guardians.

He appears to enjoy solving puzzles, particularly a Rubik's Cube. He frequently talks about his parents, but neither he nor his aunt or uncle have spoken about Dr. Connors or his experiments as of yet.

He has an adamant dislike of brussels sprouts, and his favorite subject in school is science (a possible concern . . . or a possible benefit for our company's future?).

There is no saying what type of a threat he will pose to Oscorp as he grows older.

I recommend we continue surveillance for the immediate future.

OSCORP
INDUSTRIES

EXCERPT FROM PETER PARKER SURVEILLANCE LOG—MIDTOWN HIGH SCHOOL GRADUATION

As has been his customary habit, Parker is late. He is not with his classmates on the stage.

May Parker is his only attendee in the crowd. She is looking around for her nephew, a concerned expression on her face.

Gwen Stacy, Oscorp intern and Parker's girlfriend, also appears to be searching for the offending teenager. Stacy has a record of being quite punctual at her internship with us. No doubt she is frustrated with such an irresponsible companion.

I plan to wait here for his arrival. Pretty certain he has overslept or has gotten lost or has procrastinated in some other ridiculous way customary to his age group.

~~This has to be the most boring job in Oscorp Security.~~

OSCORP

INDUSTRIES

EXCERPT FROM PETER PARKER SURVEILLANCE LOG—
MIDTOWN HIGH SCHOOL GRADUATION—CONT'D.

Gwen Stacy is the valedictorian of Midtown High.
She is inappropriately talking on her cell phone—
probably inquiring about Parker's ETA. Stacy is
being called to the podium.

Stacy is now giving her speech. Besides pondering
aloud whether Principal Conway is naked under his
gown, it is well-crafted and getting a rousing
response from the crowd. She is encouraging the
students to make their lives count for something,
to fight for what matters to them. This is quite
inspiring.

Given her public-speaking abilities and her
undeniable intelligence, she may prove to be an
asset to Oscorp as she continues her internship.

Parker has arrived just in time to receive his
diploma. May looks relieved. Parker seems winded.

The crowds are swarming now that the ceremony has
ended. Must relocate.

Stacy and Parker appear to be having a serious
conversation outside the restaurant.

I cannot get any closer without compromising the
mission. As usual, I will have to rely on body
language to assess what is going on. (I am lucky to
have had such rigorous Oscorp training in this very
skill.)

Stacy is distraught. She is shaking her head and
crying.

Parker tries to comfort her. He hugs her awkwardly.

It seems Parker is terminating their relationship.

~~What an idiot.~~

FILE PHOTO
SUBJECT: MAY
PARKER

Menken:

Attached is the most recent background check on Peter Parker's guardian, May Parker.

Here are the highlights: Since her husband's death, May Parker has been taking out more loans. Her bank, ███████████████████████, has recommended that she take out a second mortgage on her home in Forest Hills, Queens.

She has also begun attending nursing school. As you know, she has been a waitress for many years. According to our most recent studies, other folks in her demographic are transitioning into retirement instead of picking up more work.

Given all this, it is evident the Parker household is experiencing financial hardship, particularly with Peter Parker attending college in the fall.

As we know, desperate situations cause people to take desperate actions. While I understand the frustrations of the Oscorp security team assigned to this case, it is my recommendation that we continue to watch the Parker household, with perhaps a slight reduction in field time.

Call me to discuss.

Best,

████████████████████████

OSCORP
INDUSTRIES

EXCERPT FROM PETER PARKER SURVEILLANCE LOG (YEAR XX)—FOREST HILLS, QUEENS

Parker and his aunt are going through the motions of their morning routine.

Parker is rushing. He is (once again) late for his college class. ~~I am considering leaving a watch for him at the door as an anonymous gift, just so I do not have to witness this ridiculous mayhem every day.~~

May Parker has just finished yet another shift working as a nurse at the hospital.

May has packed Parker a large sack lunch. (It appears his appetite has not waned, though he is past his teenage years. He still, however, does not like brussels sprouts.)

Parker is almost out the door when May tosses the car keys to him.

EXCERPT FROM HARRY OSBORN SURVEILLANCE LOG (YEAR XX)—COASTAL HIGHWAY, CALIFORNIA

Upon the recent request of Donald Menken, we will be surveying Norman Osborn's son, Harry, heir to the Oscorp dynasty.

Unlike his father, Osborn does not seem to care about the Oscorp name.

He has been traveling to exotic locations, joyriding in sports cars, and traipsing around with supermodels since I have been observing him. He seems to have no sense of responsibility, or regard for his father's status.

He has not visited his father in years. It is evident he is content to spend his father's money without putting any effort into earning it.

At this very moment, Osborn is speeding around the edge of a coastal cliff with a terrified model clinging to her seatbelt in the front seat.

In light of Norman Osborn's illness, this does not bode well for the future of the company.

EXCERPT FROM HARRY OSBORN SURVEILLANCE LOG (YEAR XX)—COASTAL HIGHWAY, CALIFORNIA—CONT'D.

The time has come.

Norman Osborn, CEO of Oscorp Industries, is dying. This could not have happened at a worse moment, particularly while we are still under public scrutiny in the wake of Dr. Connors's "breach of trust."

I am hoping the PR team has been working on our official statement. It will have to be good.

Menken has been tasked with relaying the news to Harry Osborn. He has arrived by helicopter.

At first, Osborn is quite terse with Menken. It is evident he wants nothing to do with his father or Oscorp.

However, as soon as Menken delivers the unfortunate news, Osborn joins him in the helicopter. They are no doubt traveling back to New York to be at Norman's bedside.

We must now prepare for ~~the young spoiled ruffian~~ Harry Osborn to take over Oscorp.

~~God help us.~~

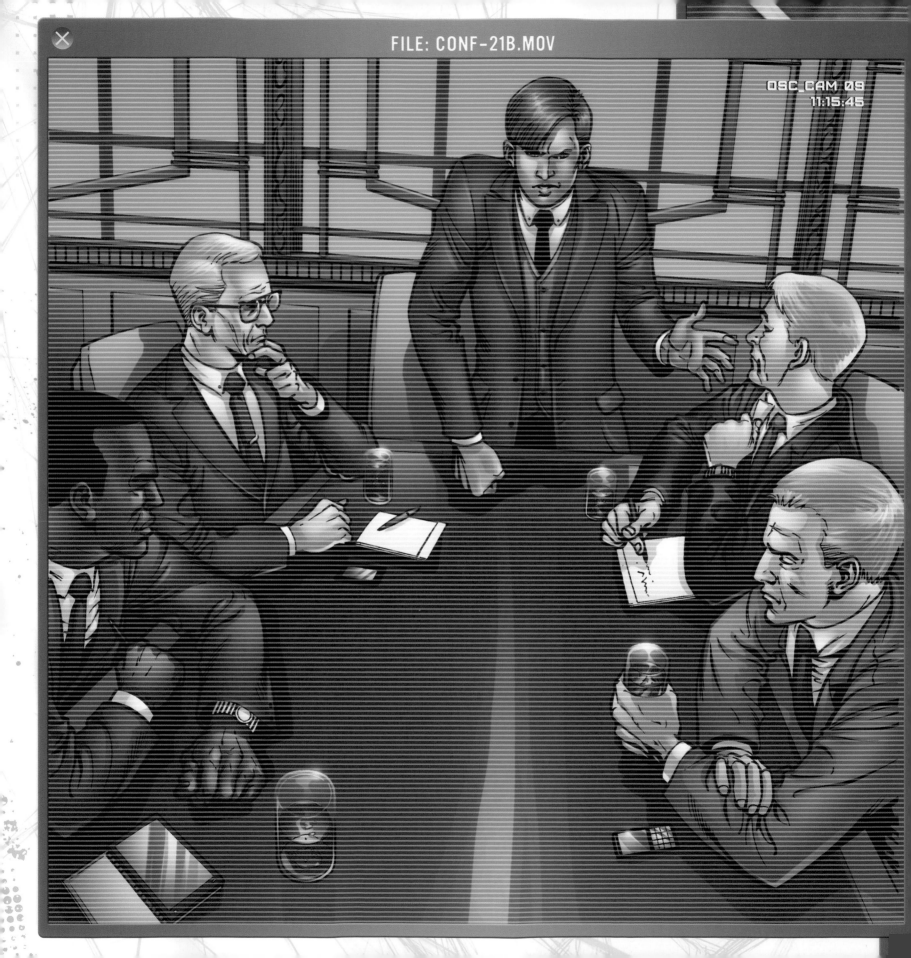

From: Donald Menken
To: ▬▬▬▬▬▬, ▬▬▬▬▬▬, ▬▬▬▬▬▬, ▬▬▬▬▬▬, ▬▬▬▬▬▬, ▬▬▬▬▬▬, ▬▬▬▬▬▬
Date: ▬▬▬▬▬▬▬▬

All:

As you know, Harry Osborn held his first meeting with the Oscorp Board this afternoon.

To say things did not go as planned would be an understatement. We were all prepared to handle the transition as smoothly as possible. It was our belief Osborn would welcome our control and direction so he could go back to spending his father's money without a responsibility or care in the world.

Instead of being compliant, Osborn proved to be surprisingly aggressive. Right after he was warned that much of the public scrutiny of the company would fall on him, he threatened to lay off anybody who did not comply with the way he ran things (quite a dangerous outlook, to say the least).

Of course, Osborn has also appointed Felicia as his personal assistant, demonstrating there is still some of the old Harry left in him.

This does not bode well. I will schedule a regrouping with the team ASAP.

Best,

Menken

**EXCERPT FROM HARRY OSBORN [AND PETER PARKER]
SURVEILLANCE LOG (YEAR XX)—UPPER WEST SIDE**

Peter Parker met with Harry Osborn today. The two
had not seen each other for eight years.

The meeting appeared to be awkward at first, with
Parker offering his condolences to Osborn for his
father's demise.

But after a brief exchange of banter (Osborn teasing
Parker about his unibrow, and Parker teasing Osborn
about his hair being blow-dried by servants [Note:
have not witnessed this to be true]), the two got
along surprisingly well.

They moved their reunion to the Hudson River on
Harry's new speedboat. After about ninety minutes,
they parked the boat at a nearby pier in Queens and
started walking alongside the river. This is where
they are now.

I have been unable to get close enough to hear their
conversation since they've been at the river, but
they seem to be enjoying each other's company. There
seems to be some laughter and some more serious,
earnest conversation. No doubt they are recalling
memories of their childhood and speaking of their
fathers.

Given their fathers' relationship, there is no telling whether this renewed friendship will be good or bad for the future of Oscorp.

SPIDER-MAN: TIES TO THE RUSSIAN MAFIA?

Story by Brittany Candau • Photography by Peter Parker

Masked fiend Spider-Man made another public appearance Saturday in the midst of a high-speed chase.

Authorities were pursuing notorious Russian Mafia criminal Aleksei Sytsevich, who had hijacked an Oscorp truck. The truck contained canisters of deadly plutonium.

After a seventy-four-block chase, NYPD and SWAT vehicles were closing in on the criminal when Spider-Man suddenly appeared out of nowhere. He used his "webs" to swing from car to car, attempting to reach Sytsevich first.

How does he do this?

"It was clear he wanted to get to the van before the police. Who knows? Maybe he wanted to distract them or something," said a source close to the investigation.

Moments later, Spider-Man did in fact reach the stolen van. According to eyewitnesses, he even appeared to have a casual conversation with Sytsevich while hanging off the side of the vehicle.

Spider-Man then webbed up the canisters of plutonium that were suddenly being hurled from the back of the van, stopping them from crashing to the ground. A line of police vehicles forced the van to stop.

At that moment, Sytsevich's men started firing their weapons. Spider-Man webbed the guns out of the criminals' hands, along with the remaining canisters of plutonium that started to fall out of the van.

Meanwhile, an armed Sytsevich jumped out of the van. Spider-Man dodged his bullets (a little *too* easily, some say) and then webbed the criminal mastermind to some posts, grabbing the remaining plutonium as he disarmed Sytsevich.

Look into this.

It is unclear whether these two men have met before. But some speculate they could even be working together.

Cont'd. on page A5.

et PR
m
this
ediately.

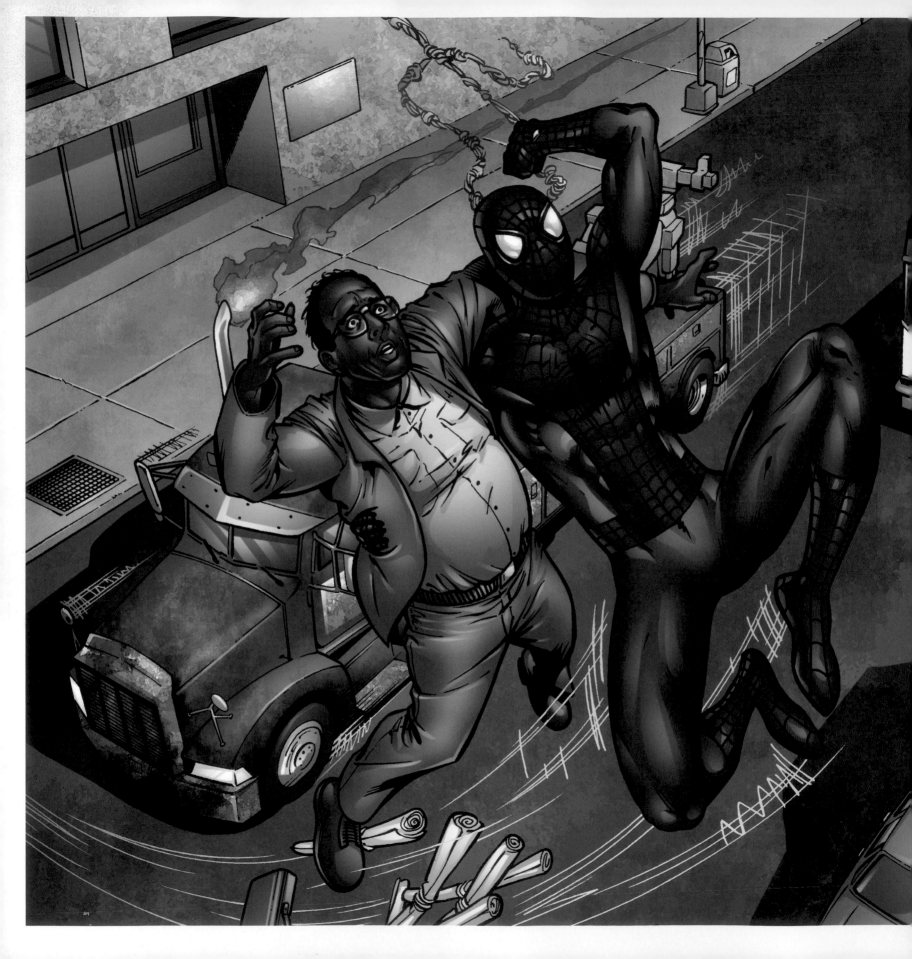

"Sure, Spider-Man stopped the truck and made sure that the plutonium didn't explode, and Sytsevich was stopped—or whatever," said an expert on Mafia dealings. "But what if this was all part of a more elaborate plan between Sytsevich and the Spider? It wouldn't be too difficult for Spider-Man to break Sytsevich out of prison with those freaky abilities of his. And the two seemed pretty chummy."

Adding to the rising suspicion, Spider-Man fled the scene before authorities arrested Sytsevich and his men.

Who is Spider-Man?

Does SM have connection to research done by ███████

OSCORP EMPLOYEE REVIEW

Employee: Max Dillon
Division: Chemical Genomics Lab
Direct Report: Alistair Smythe
Title: Electrical Engineer

Review:

Dillon is often late. He has been warned that he needs to be more punctual, lest he be terminated.

While Dillon provides adequate work in the lab and on the power grid, he does not really stand out. He is, for all intents and purposes, competent, but clearly not an all-star employee.

He is usually quiet and unimpressive. He occasionally brings up delusional ideas that *he* came up with our division's best breakthroughs, including my hydropower plan. Clearly, he is not a team player and would not do well working closely with others.

Dillon is best suited for remaining in his current position: maintaining the lab equipment on his own.

Electrical engineer Max Dillon was compromised in a lab accident yesterday. It cannot be stressed enough that this was due to his own negligence and is in no way the company's fault.

Dillon was warned of a malfunction in sector 5A. It appears he attempted to reconnect the circuit source above the power tank filled with electric eels. He was balanced precariously above said tank while tinkering with the system. This obviously goes against his training.

Upon reconnecting the circuit (**and without first turning the power off— again, Oscorp is not liable**), Dillon was shocked with electricity. He then fell into the tank with the electric eels.

Dillon's body has been taken to an unknown location. Awaiting further instructions on Oscorp's plan of action.

FILE: B02_01A.MOV

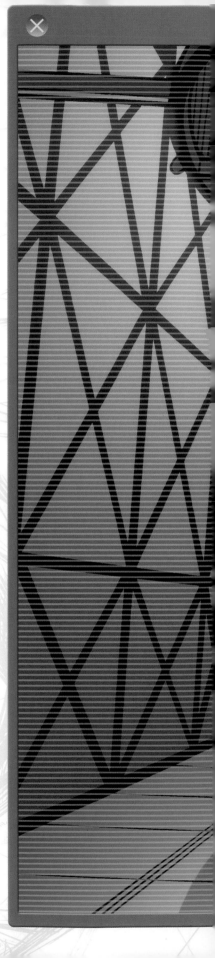

NO GO FOR ELECTRO!

Story by Tomas Palacios• Photography by Peter Parker

ka Max
illon.
must make
ure his
dentity
nd
onnection
o Oscorp
re not
eaked!

Spider-Man regained popular favor last night by defeating a new super-powered threat to the city, a glowing fiend dubbed "Electro."

It is unclear where Electro (or his ability to shoot deadly shock waves of electricity) has come from. Good.

What *is* known is that around 7:30 P.M. last night, Electro unveiled his powers of destruction in Times Square. The glowing fiend used his electrical waves to flip a delivery truck in the middle of the street.

As police officers, firefighters, and SWAT team members gathered, Electro held his hands in front of him, seemingly intent on electrocuting as many civilians and authorities as possible.

Who is this guy?

Finally, Spider-Man swung in on his webs, attempting to negotiate with Electro. Predictably, the villain would not have any of this. He threw a police vehicle at the masked hero, and seemed to shock him.

Electro then started to fire bolts into the air, causing a nearby building to shed debris toward the tourists below. Spider-Man recovered, jumping into action to save a man from being crushed and a couple of tourists from being electrocuted on the TKTS bleachers, which were

Cont'd. on page A3.

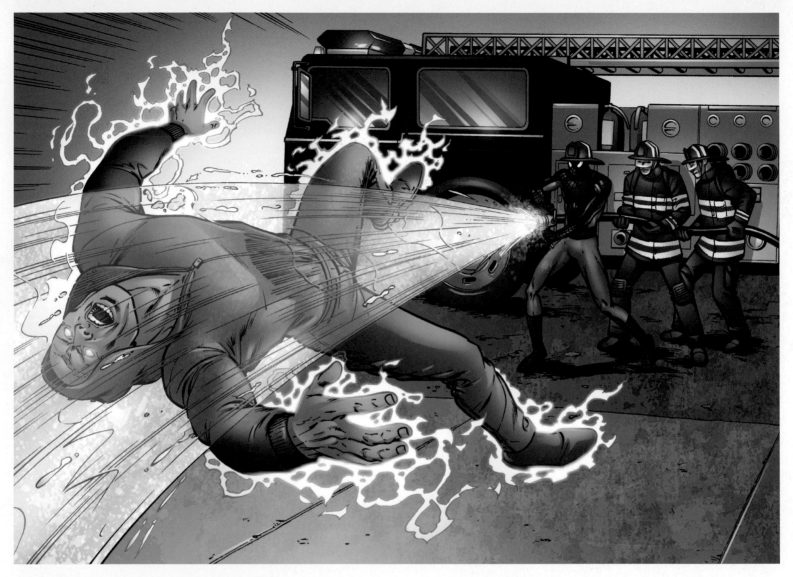

Spider-Man and the NYFD take down Electro.

also compromised by another one of Electro's deadly energy waves.

This reporter would be remiss if he didn't mention that Spider-Man made a critical error in propelling a hydrant at the villain. It threw Electro into the massive jumbotrons surrounding the scene, and the electrical explosion only seemed to fuel Electro. The super-powered figure rose into the air, laughing maniacally as he floated over the scene.

Luckily, this terror was short-lived. Spider-Man and two firefighters blasted Electro with a fire hose. The water quelled the villain, who was promptly taken into custody by the authorities.

RAVENCROFT

RAVENCROFT INSTITUTE

PATIENT ID: 696

PHYSICIAN: DR. KAFKA

NOTES:

Patient has undergone an indeterminable amount of electric shock. His exposure to the electric eels while he was undergoing severe electrocution seems to have both saved his life and produced extreme side effects.

Said side effects include strong electrical currents pulsing through his body and out of his extremities as well as an aversion to water. It appears his complete internal makeup has been changed. His body now appears to be powered completely by electricity. His pulse only grows stronger when charged with more electricity.

Patient also appears to be physically stronger and more outspoken than he ever was as Max Dillon based on our surveillance loggings from when he worked at Oscorp Industries.

Further studies to begin immediately.

RAVENCROFT INSTITUTE LAB REPORT

My first interaction with Patient 696, who refers to himself as "Electro," was very illuminating (forgive the pun).

Electro immediately recognized the military-grade bio-stem electrodes we are treating him with. It is evident he has retained memories of his former life as Max Dillon. Quite a fascinating development, given the significant shock he experienced in both a physiological and psychological sense.

The subject became more and more worked up as I spoke with him, showing a significant spike in brain activity.

Making threats to absorb all the power in the city, Electro attempted to demonstrate his potency by shattering a light bulb and my glasses.

However, as soon as we lowered him into the tank, we made it clear who was, in fact, in charge of the experiment.

I anticipate more information regarding this patient and his new abilities in the upcoming weeks.

Results will be documented accordingly.

EXCERPT FROM HARRY OSBORN (AND PETER PARKER) SURVEILLANCE LOG (YEAR XX)—UPPER WEST SIDE

Parker is visiting Osborn at the office. The two are becoming quite chummy as of late. It certainly feels like the old days with Richard and Norman being inseparable.

Osborn shows Parker the new military body-armor prototype. Let the record show that Osborn has been warned repeatedly not to share such top secret projects with anybody. He is as reckless as ever.

Parker demonstrated his admittedly vast knowledge and expertise in the technology used in the suit, inquiring about the use of servomotors and whether it was polymetric or carbon. Parker might actually be a great employee at Oscorp if he were at all punctual or showed any inclination toward being responsible. Hmmm. I now see why he and Osborn get along so well.

Osborn then went into details about the suit, explaining how it can heal battlefield injuries.

I'm actually pretty impressed with the feats we at Oscorp have accomplished for the good of all mankind. ~~Besides the whole Dr. Connors wreaking havoc on the city as a murderous lizard thing, of course.~~

EXCERPT FROM HARRY OSBORN (AND PETER PARKER) SURVEILLANCE LOG (YEAR XX)—OSCORP

Osborn has closed his office door. I am once again relying on reading body language through the glass windows of his office. (I do not get paid enough for this job.)

It appears that Osborn is getting more and more upset. Parker looks concerned. I am assuming Osborn has just informed Parker that he is suffering from the same genetic disease that his father had.

In short, that he is dying.

Osborn is showing Parker something on his monitor. Perhaps information about his father's work to cure the disease? We will have to go into his computer's history when he exits the office to learn more.

Now, strangely enough, Osborn is holding up a copy of The Daily Bugle. There is a front-page article about Spider-Man. Parker looks downright alarmed.

Osborn is gesturing emphatically. Parker seems angry. Using my (significant) detection abilities, I believe Osborn thinks the masked hero is somehow the key to his cure. He is most likely reaching out to Parker because he takes all those photographs of Spider-Man for the newspaper.

OSCORP

I almost feel sorry for Osborn. This has to be a
last resort on his part. There's no way that Parker
would actually know the identity and/or whereabouts
of Spider-Man. He simply has a camera with a
great long lens. Even nicer than the cameras our
department has. (Clearly it is time for an upgrade!)

Parker is leaving. Things seem to have cooled down
between the friends. Now they both just look sad.

WARNING: POTENTIAL SECURITY BREACH!
WARNING: POTENTIAL SECURITY BREACH!

Computer ID: I9287008

User: Gwen Stacy, Intern

Search history using trigger words:

Max Dillon

Max Dillan

Max Dilon

Max Dillon hydropower

Electrical engineer hydropower

Chemical Genomics Lab Max Dillon

Threat level: **HIGH**

Recommended course of action: detain user for questioning immediately, ensuring that he/she does not know incriminating information about Special Projects and discouraging any further searches on related topics.

EXCERPT FROM HARRY OSBORN SURVEILLANCE LOG (YEAR XX)—UPPER WEST SIDE

Osborn had a surprising visitor tonight: Spider-Man! The wall-crawler must have heard through the grapevine that Osborn was looking for him. He is no doubt very well connected to the goings-on of the rich and powerful in the city.

Embarrassingly, Osborn was in an unflattering state when Spider-Man entered his living room. Osborn appeared disheveled, sleep deprived, and insufferably argumentative. He offered Spider-Man a large sum for helping him.

Spider-Man would not take Osborn's money. He said he did not want to put Osborn in danger. But he would try to find "another way" to help him.
Osborn did not take well to this. He threw a glass at the hero and attempted to fight him.

To his credit, Spider-Man did not get angry. He simply swung out the window and away from the scene.

Osborn is now screaming, "It's not fair!" over and over again at the top of his lungs.

Things have gotten quite tense. I think I need a coffee break.

From: Donald Menken

To: ██████████, ████████████, ██████████, ████████, ██████████

Date: ██████████

All:

I want to provide a quick recap regarding the events from today.

As you undoubtedly know by now, Osborn was let go. The idea was to wait another month or so before enacting this phase of the plan. However, his insubordination, along with his most recent actions, which clearly demonstrate a desperate man in a downward spiral, left us with no other option but to fire him early.

He has been made aware of the Special Projects/Electro situation. He also knows that if he tries to fight his termination, we will inform the public that not only was he aware of Max Dillon's accident, but he was the one to authorize the cover-up.

Not surprisingly, Osborn was worked up by this turn of events. He does not like that we have outsmarted him from the beginning, and that he was too careless to really look at what was going on in his company. Security had to escort Osborn out of the building.

We will have a debriefing tomorrow to discuss the next course of action. Please be assured that I have no concerns about his causing any trouble for us at this time.

Best,

Menken

RAVENCROFT

Ravencroft Institute Security

Gate 4

Visitor: Harry Osborn, CEO

Notes: Mr. Osborn was not on the list but insisted on entering the facility. He would not let Frank call his supervisor to make sure it was okay. After Mr. Osborn threatened to fire Frank, it seemed prudent for Frank to let him in.

Mr. Osborn also stated that he needed to see a certain inmate in the isolation wing. He did not share the patient's name. He wanted Frank to take him to the wing personally.

Frank opened the gate and led Mr. Osborn into the facility.

We are to await further instructions from either Frank or Mr. Osborn here at Gate 4.

RAVENCROFT

WARNING: SECURITY BREACH!
WARNING: SECURITY BREACH!

Calling all security units to maximum-security wing immediately! Harry Osborn has infiltrated the room of patient 696, aka Electro.

Osborn is armed with a Taser gun and has already tased two guards in front of the wing to unconsciousness.

Note: Osborn is the one who pulled the fire alarm in an effort to distract the staff. **There are no fires or gas leaks compromising the building at this time.**

Osborn is also no longer the acting CEO of Oscorp and should be detained immediately.

All units—proceed quickly and cautiously.

FILE: NW33_RAV.MOV

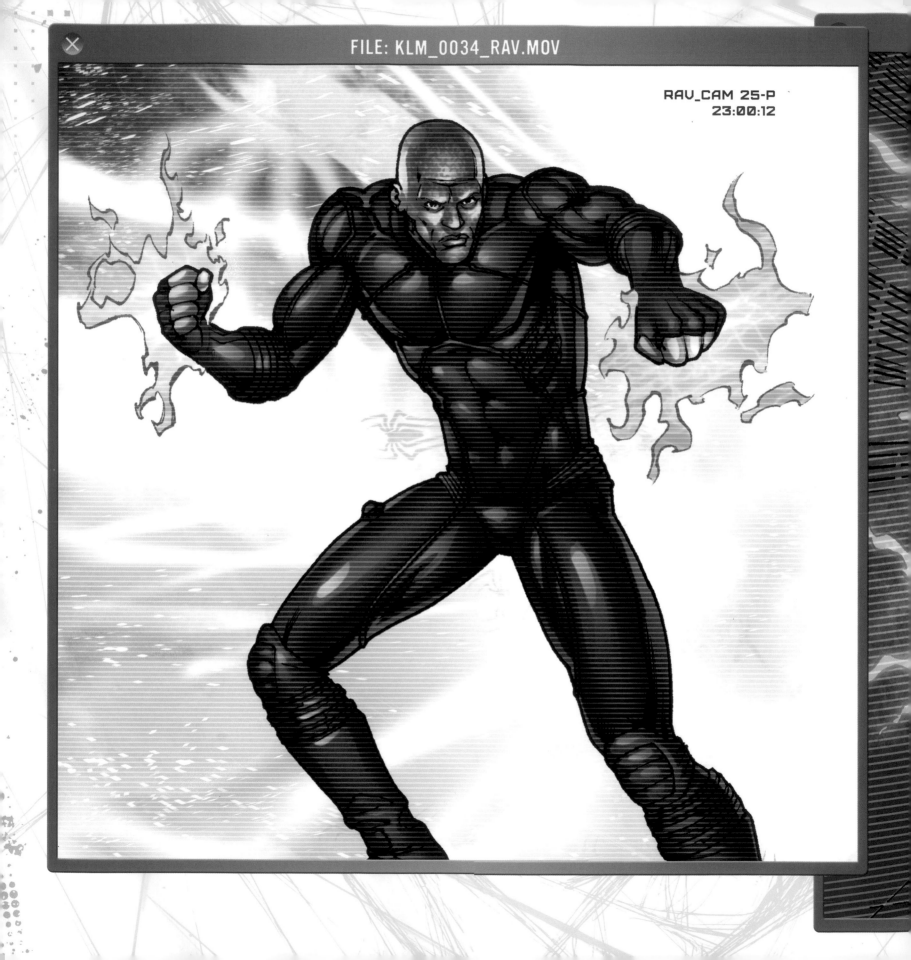

RAV_CAM 25-P
23:00:12

RAV_CAM 8C
23:45:10

From: ▮▮▮▮▮▮▮
To: ▮▮▮▮▮▮▮
Date: ▮▮▮▮▮▮▮

I have been trying to reach you at your work and cell-phone numbers for the last half hour. We've had a situation here at Ravencroft that needs your immediate attention.

Shortly before our security heads received the news of Harry Osborn's termination, he convinced our guards to let him in.

Using a combination of threats and a Taser, Osborn made his way to our most deadly patient, Electro. He used the aforementioned Taser to charge the patient with electricity, which made the patient strong enough to break free of his restraints.

The patient then managed to take out twelve Ravencroft guards with his electric bolts.

It appears Osborn and Electro left the facility together. We do not know where they are going or what end they are working toward. It is obvious, however, that it is not good.

Call me immediately to discuss a plan of action.

Best,

▮▮▮▮▮▮▮▮▮▮▮▮

NYPD 911 EMERGENCY CALL TRANSCRIPT

Date: ▇▇▇▇▇▇▇▇▇

Incoming phone number: ▇▇▇▇▇▇▇▇▇▇▇

Operator: 911, what's your emergency?

Caller: That glowing guy from the news! Electro! He's here! I see him.

Operator: Where do you see him, sir?

Caller: He just . . . I don't know . . . he sort of *flew* past me. He's got all these crazy sparks coming off of him.

Operator: Where are you, sir?

Caller: I'm next to the power plant. I can see him up there. I think I heard him say he was going to take away all the power in the city!

Operator: Which power plant? Do you see a street sign nearby?

Caller: This is crazy. I just took a picture with my cell phone. I can text it to you. I'm . . . Whoa.

Operator: Sir? Hello? Sir? Are you still there?

End of transcript

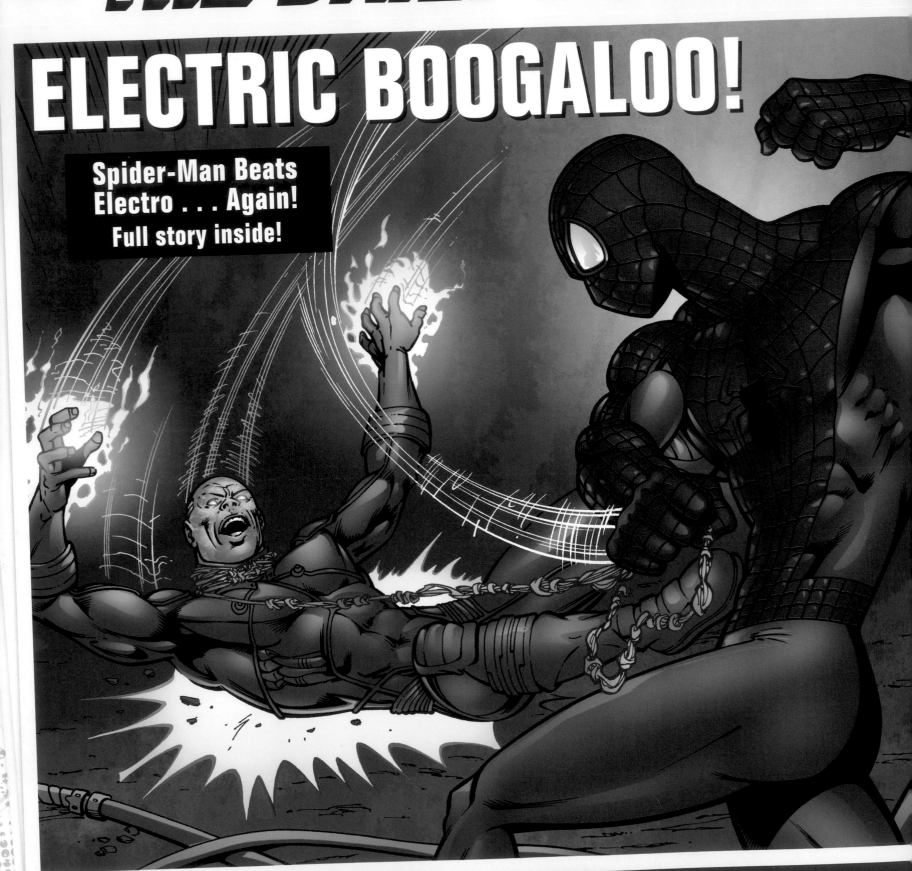

SPIDER-MAN "AMPS" UP HIS GAME: BRINGS POWER BACK TO NYC

Story by Clarissa Wong • Photography by Peter Parker

It was only weeks ago that electrically charged villain Electro was put behind bars at the Ravencroft Institute for the Criminally Insane. However, in a strange twist of events, the psychotic criminal escaped the institute last night and attempted to steal the power in New York City. He may have succeeded if Spider-Man hadn't stepped in once again.

Details about the confrontation are still hazy. We do know that Electro managed to break free from Ravencroft in the early evening hours. Oscorp employees declined to comment on how the criminal escaped from the maximum-security wing of the facility.

Electro made his way to a local power plant, using his electric bolts to cause a massive citywide blackout. Businesses, residences, and—even more crucially—hospitals were significantly affected.

"It was terrifying," said a local nurse. "We usually have backup generators in case of power outages so our patients can be cared for during emergencies. But the backup generators wouldn't turn on. We were afraid we wouldn't be able to get critical life-saving machines back up and running."

According to eyewitnesses close to the plant, Spider-Man webbed his way to the scene shortly after the blackout occurred. The two super-powered beings battled—Electro with his electric surges, and Spider-Man with his webs. What happened next is still unclear.

"They just sort of disappeared from view," said one bystander. "One minute, we're witnessing Spider-Man confronting Electro. The next—poof. They're out of sight."

Cont'd. on page A2.

[Handwritten margin notes:]

need ...sue ...fficial ...ement his N.

We need to know what happened here. Collect any surveillance footage from the power plant.

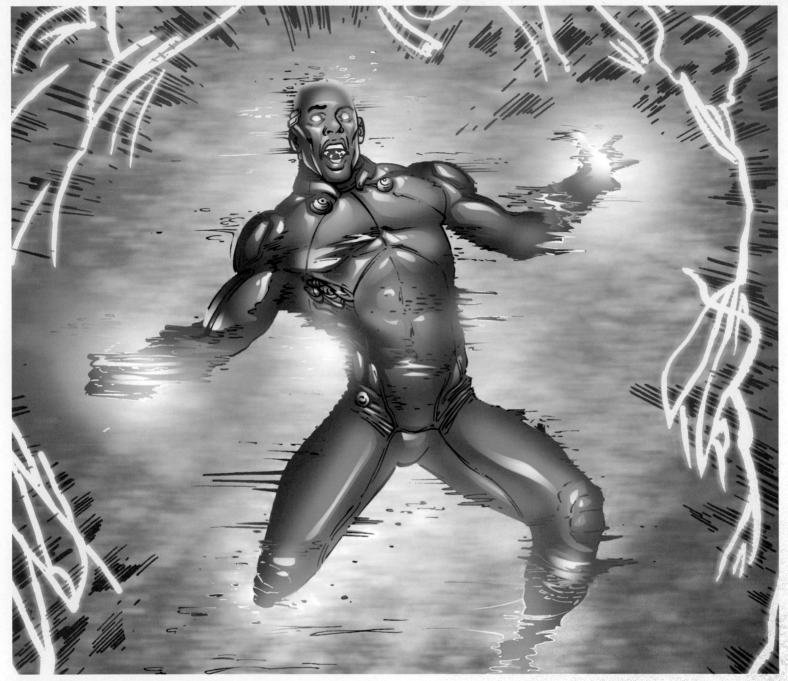

Spider-Man neutralizes the situation.

It is still not yet known how exactly Spider-Man stopped Electro, or what has even happened to the volatile fiend. What *is* clear is that power was restored to the city within the next fifteen minutes, and Spider-Man was seen swinging away from the scene.

No word yet on whether Electro is back in custody. As usual, we could not reach Spider-Man for comment.

We have more questions than answers regarding the masked hero known as Spider-Man. He could prove to be a threat to Oscorp. He could prove to be an asset. It's crucial that we collect more information to determine which so we can proceed accordingly.

Immediate questions regarding Spider-Man:

• Who is he?

• How is he connected to Oscorp (if at all)?

• Where did he come from?

• When/where can I speak with him?

• Why is he here?

• Who is he working with?

• What is the extent of his powers?

• What is his end goal?